This Book is Given With Love 

To

____

From

____

Camden And His Superpower Ears

Go To A New School

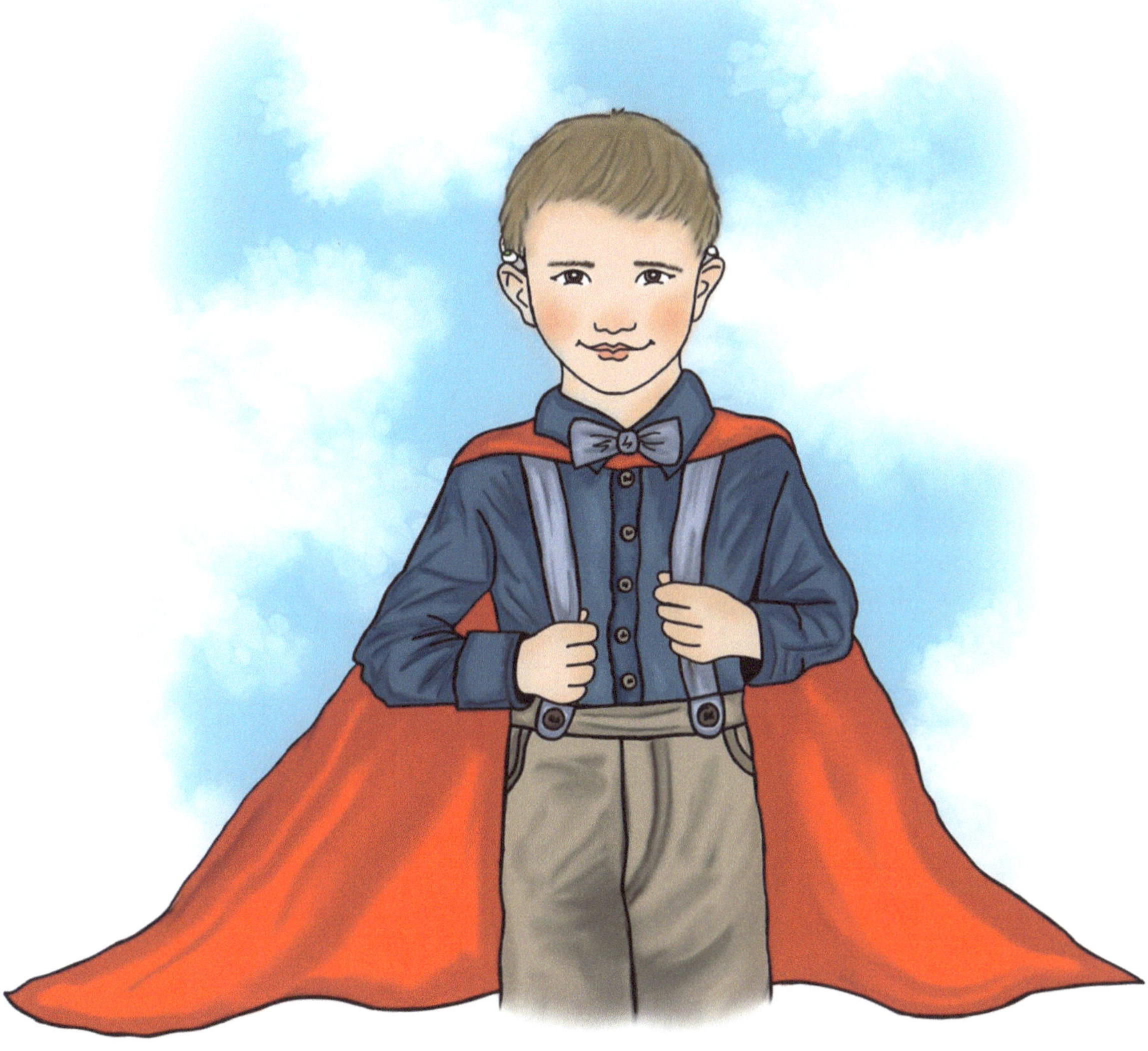

Written by Leigh Porter Cutrone

Illustrated by Madeleine Davis

ISBN 978-1-958032-08-4 (Hardcover Edition)
ISBN 978-1-958032-04-6 (Paperback Edition)

Registered in the Library of Congress.

Cover Design and Illustrations by Madeleine Davis
Page Composition by Levi Stephen – 303 Pixels LLC (303pixels.com)

Printed in the United States of America.

Published by Here I Am Publishing, LLC.
info@hereiampublishingllc.com
Sandi Huddleston-Edwards, Publisher
780 Monterrosa Drive
Myrtle Beach, SC 29572

Dedication

This book is dedicated to my grandson, Camden, who
reminds us just how wonderfully unique and special
we all are and for showing us all that deafness does not
have to stop anyone from following their dreams.

Acknowledgements

First and foremost, I want to thank my husband who has
encouraged me throughout the process of writing this book.
He is my motivating and supportive partner in all that I do.

Thank you also to all of my friends and family who have
given me their critiques with kindness and to my wonderful
grandchildren (Camden, Crew, Lenox, Lucy, and Fiona)
who, with all their child-like excitement and enthusiasm
about this book, helped me see the finish line!

Camden woke up in his new bedroom
just in time to see the sun peeking through his window.

Today was the day Camden would be going to a new school!
Brandy barked and jumped up onto Camden's bed.
He wagged his tail and gave Camden a big dog kiss.
YUCK!

His mommy came in and gave Camden a wake-up hug. Camden
couldn't hear his mommy talking or Brandy barking.
All was quiet — very quiet — as it was every morning for Camden.
He couldn't hear anything at all until he put on his special *ears*.

Camden jumped out of bed and smiled excitedly, while he
attached batteries to his *ears*. He slipped them on, placing each of
the two magnets on precisely the right spots above both his ears.
All set! Now he could hear!

"Good morning!" Mommy said. "It's going to be a busy day. Are you excited about your new school?"

"Yes," Camden answered, but he was very nervous. Butterflies were in his tummy. He already knew he would be the only one in his class who wore these *ears*.

After breakfast, Camden was all ready to go to school.
"Bye, Buddy. Have a great day!" his daddy yelled as he opened
the front door. "Bye, Daddy!" called Camden.
Mommy and Camden jumped into the car, and away they went.

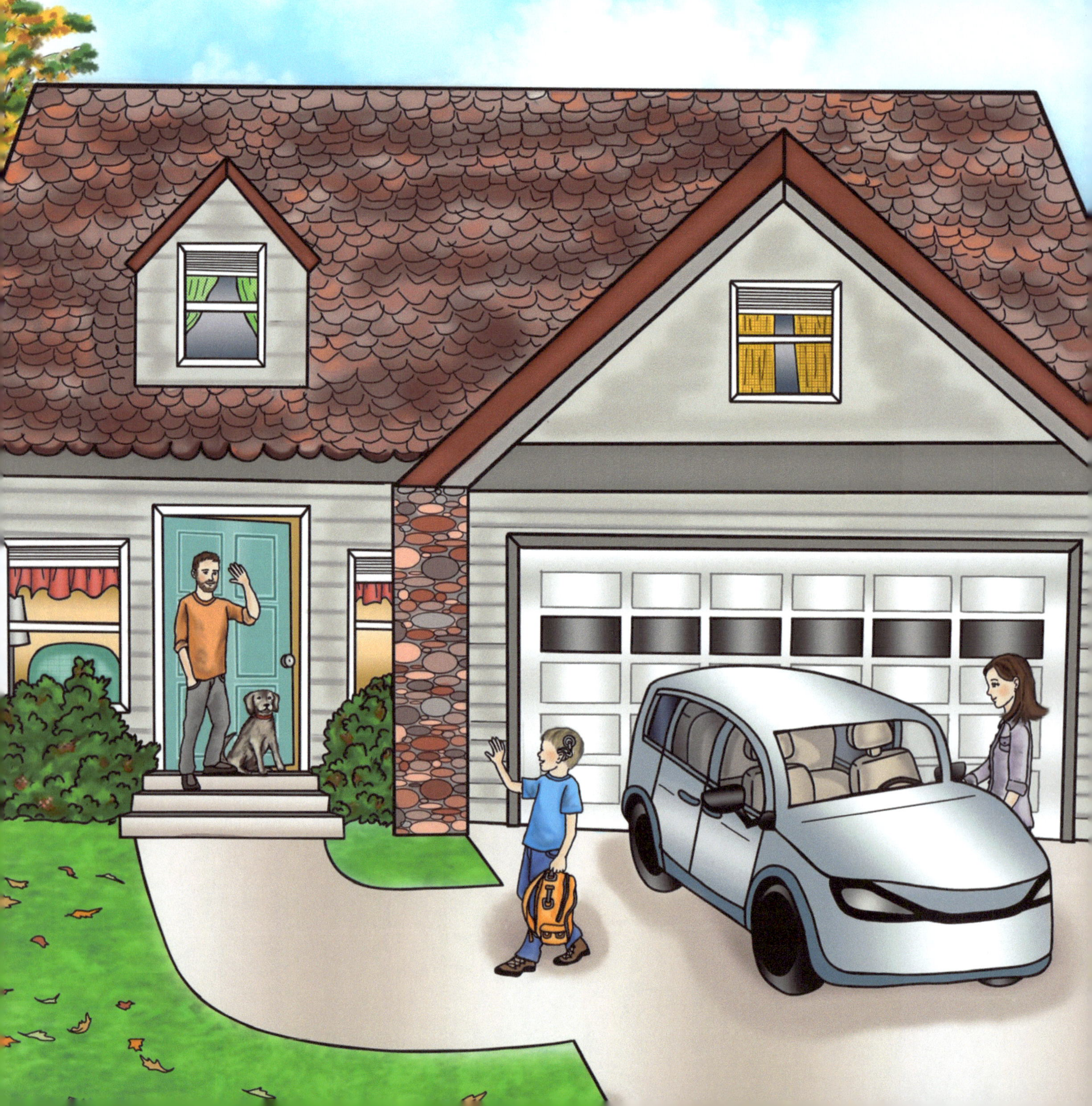

At the school, Camden and his mommy met Principal Sneezer,
who was waiting for them in his office.
"Welcome, Camden!" Mr. Sneezer said.
"Thank you," Camden replied.

As they walked toward his new classroom, Camden wondered if anyone had ever seen a person with *ears* like his. He knew he would have to explain them to his new classmates.
Would they all stare at him?

Camden's new teacher, Miss Tickle, came to the door and greeted
his mommy and welcomed Camden to her classroom.
His mommy hugged him and said, "I'll see you after school."
Miss Tickle seemed nice. Camden followed her
into the classroom.

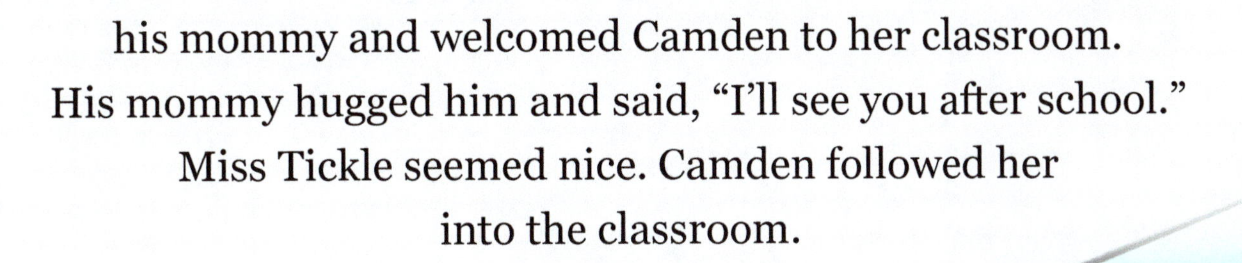

Miss Tickle introduced Camden to the class.
"This is Camden! He is brand-new to our school."
The students stopped what they were doing and looked
at Camden and his *ears*.

"Miss Tickle, what is on Camden's head?"
a girl named Susie asked.
A boy named Bobby giggled and said,
"I NEVER saw anything like THOSE before!"

"These are Camden's second set of *ears* so he can hear,"
Miss Tickle answered Susie. "He cannot hear without them."
"He has SUPERPOWER EARS? SO COOL!" Bobby yelled.
Everyone agreed and smiled at Camden. Camden's *ears* had
superpower! Camden began to relax, thinking that explaining his
ears might not be so bad.

Miss Tickle turned and asked Camden,
"May I tell the class about your superpower *ears*?"
Camden smiled and replied, "Thanks, but I'd like to tell everybody
about them myself if that's OK."
Miss Tickle was surprised and pleased Camden wanted to show
and tell about his unique *ears*.

"When I was born," Camden explained, "I could not hear. So, the doctors gave me my superpower *ears* when I was two-and-a-half years-old. If everyone talks to me at the same time, it is hard for me to understand. Whenever this green light is bright, they are working. If I play hide-and-seek at night, friends find me easily!"
Bobby yelled, "Hey, that's not fair!" Everyone giggled.
Camden continued. "I charge my batteries at night, and the *ears* go into a drying box."

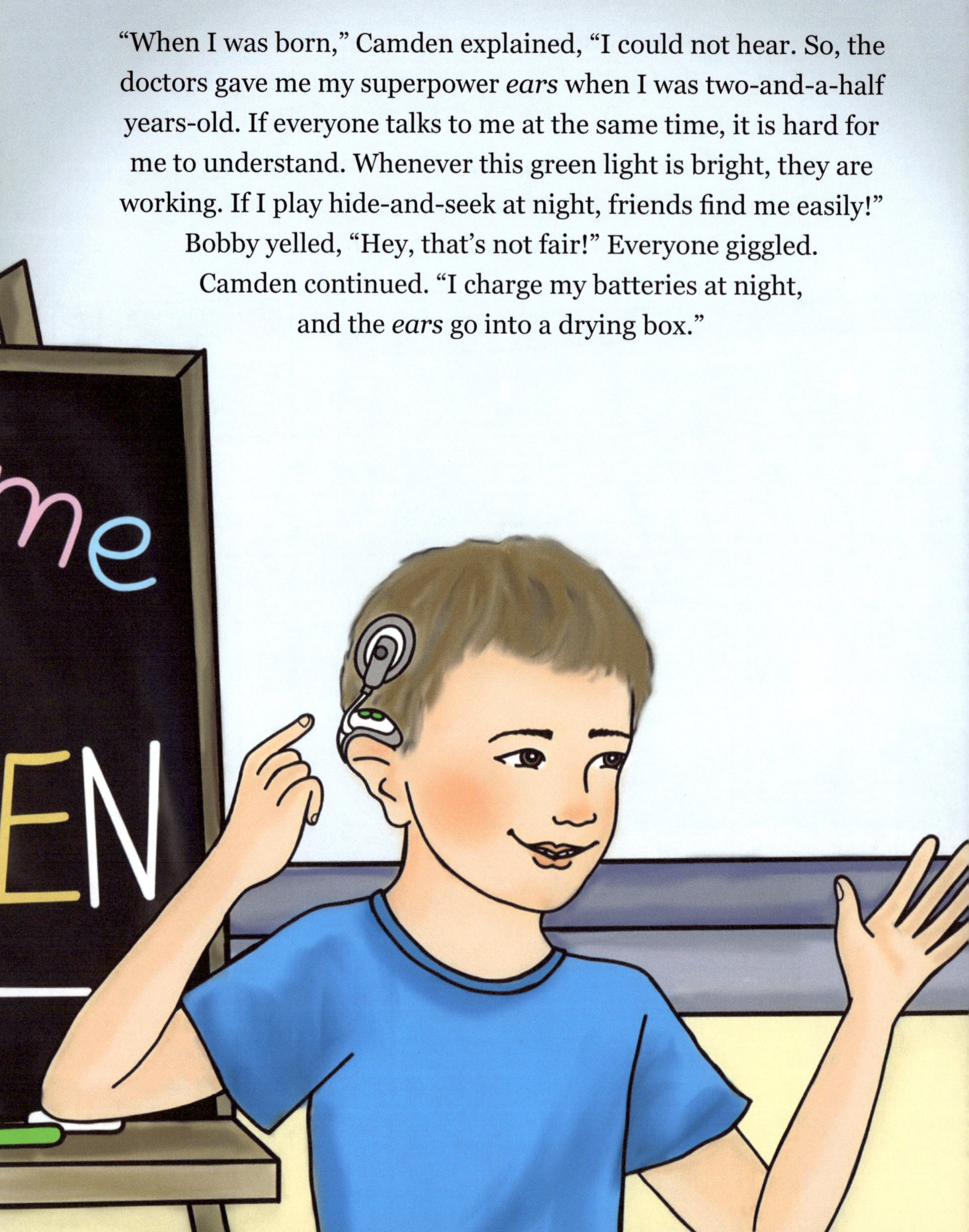

"Now, children," Miss Tickle said, "I want you to look at me and not talk. We are going to play a game. I will talk and everyone will listen to me. First, cover your ears and stay quiet."
The class covered their ears while looking at the teacher. It became very, very quiet. Miss Tickle began to talk, but no one could hear her. A moment later, Miss Tickle motioned for the students to uncover their ears.

"Did anyone know what I was saying?" the teacher asked. The students looked at each other and shook their heads NO! They had not been able to hear anything at all. WOW! Miss Tickle explained this is what it's like for Camden without his superpower *ears*.

Susie raised her hand and asked, "Why can't Camden hear?"
"Each of us is different, aren't we?" asked Miss Tickle. "We are all very special and unique in so many ways. Camden happens not to hear. Can anyone think of other ways we are special?"
Susie thought about this for a moment. "I understand!" she said. "My cousin has to wear glasses because she can't see very well."
Bobby said, "My friend is in a wheelchair because he can't walk."

"Great examples, Susie and Bobby. You are both right," Miss Tickle said. "Now, don't forget class. If anyone sees Camden's *ears* come off during the day, please pick them up and give them back to him. Now, let's give Camden a happy welcome!"

Everyone jumped up and gave Camden fist bumps or high fives.
Susie gave Camden such a big hug that one of his *ears* fell off!
"Uh, oh!" said Susie. She picked it up and gave it back to Camden.
"I'm sorry." Camden quickly slipped his *ear* back on and
smiled at Susie. "No problem! Thank you!"

Bobby patted Camden on the back, and said,
"You are our SUPERPOWER friend!"

That evening at supper, Camden eagerly told his mommy and
daddy all about his great day at school.
"I told my class all about my *ears*. It was so cool!
I've made new friends, too."
Brandy sat beside Camden, listening to every word.
Bedtime came quickly, so Camden got ready for bed.

"Good night, Buddy," said Daddy.
"Lights out," whispered Mommy after giving him a goodnight kiss.
"Good night, Mommy and Daddy," said Camden. He removed his
ears and plugged the batteries into the charger. He put his *ears*
into the drying box. Camden snuggled into his cozy bed.
He could hardly wait for the next day of school!

Camden's world became quiet again. He could not hear the fire engine rushing down the street. It was quiet. He could not hear Brandy barking at people walking their dogs outside. It was quiet. He could not hear the television downstairs. Everything was quiet — very, VERY quiet.

What a GREAT day! Camden thought as he drifted off to sleep
in the peaceful quiet. Tomorrow will be another
FANTASTIC day.

About the Author
Leigh Porter Cutrone

Leigh is a Jersey girl who was born in Lakewood, New Jersey, and who graduated from Cherry Hill High School West in New Jersey. She earned a B.A. in Business Administration and Marketing from Stockton University, New Jersey.

Her favorite position was working at Harvard Law School for Professor Archibald Cox, former Watergate Special Prosecutor and who also was Solicitor General for President Kennedy. For the majority of Leigh's career, she worked as a litigation legal assistant in Houston, Texas, and Ft. Lauderdale, Florida. She also has had several of her own businesses.

She and her husband, Bob, have a daughter, son, and five precious grandchildren. When not working, they love traveling the world.

When Leigh is not with her family, she loves to write. She has a blog, *The Senior Class*, which is all about the journey of being a senior citizen. She writes children's books and also has written freelance articles for several publications.

Leigh and her husband now reside in Myrtle Beach, South Carolina.

Understanding Cochlear Implants

What is a cochlear implant?

"A cochlear implant is an implanted electronic hearing device, designed to produce useful hearing sensations to a person with severe to profound nerve deafness by electrically stimulating nerves inside the inner ear" (FDA.gov/context 2/4/2018).

When may a child receive implants?

According to the Boston Children's Hospital, a child should receive implants "as early as possible beginning at 10 to 12 months of age..." (Boston Children's Hospital).

Will an implant work for everybody?

"Most children with good language abilities, consistent listening therapy, and full-time use of the device can learn to use this sound to understand spoken language" (Boston Children's Hospital).

Will an implant restore hearing?

No, an implant will "not restore normal hearing, but they are devices that allow a child to be mainstreamed with sounds and speech processing" (Boston Children's Hospital).

How many children have cochlear implants?

"As of December 2019, approximately 736,900 cochlear implants have been implanted worldwide. In the United States, roughly 118,100 devices have been implanted in adults and 65,000 in children" (nidcd.nih.gov-health).

How many babies are born with hearing problems?

"According to the National Institute on Deafness, two to three out of every 1,000 babies are born in the U.S. have hearing defects" (National Institute on Deafness).

www.ingramcontent.com/pod-product-compliance
Lightning Source LLC
Chambersburg PA
CBHW041422300726
48981CB00007B/379